America Goes to War

The War of 1812

by Anne Todd

Consultant:
Melodie Andrews
Associate Professor of History
Minnesota State University, Mankato

CAPSTONE BOOKS
an imprint of Capstone Press
Mankato, Minnesota

Capstone Books are published by Capstone Press
151 Good Counsel Drive, P.O. Box 669, Mankato, Minnesota 56002
http://www.capstone-press.com

Library of Congress Cataloging-in-Publication Data
Todd, Anne
    The War of 1812/by Anne Todd.
    p. cm.—(America goes to war)
    Includes bibliographical references and index
    Summary: Discusses the causes, events, campaigns, personalities, and aftermath
of the War of 1812.
    ISBN 0-7368-0585-0
    1. United States—History—War of 1812—Juvenile literature. [1. United States—
History—War of 1812.] I. Title. II. Series.

E354.T64 2001
973.5'2—dc21   00-024199

Editorial Credits
Blake Hoena, editor; Timothy Halldin, cover designer and illustrator; Katy Kudela,
    photo researcher

Photo Credits
Archive Photos, 8, 12, 14, 22, 24, 26, 40
FPG International LLC, 6, 29
North Wind Photo Archives, cover, 10, 17, 19, 30, 32, 34, 37, 39

1 2 3 4 5 6 06 05 04 03 02 01

Table of Contents

Features

Fast Facts

Dates of the War: The War of 1812 lasted from June 18, 1812, to December 24, 1814. But the final battle of the war was fought January 8, 1815, after a treaty had already been signed.

Issues of the War: Great Britain was preventing U.S. trade with foreign countries. It also was impressing U.S. sailors. These sailors were forced to serve in the British Navy.

Battle Locations: Most battles occurred along the U.S. and Canadian border. Other battles occurred on the Great Lakes as well as along the Atlantic coast.

Major battles: British capture of Detroit (July 1812); *Constitution* vs. *Guerrière* (August 1812); *Chesapeake* vs. *Shannon* (June 1813); Dearborn Massacre (August 1812); Battle of Lake Erie (September 1813); Battle of the Thames (October 1813); Battle of Horseshoe Bend (March 1814); Burning of Washington, D.C. (August 1814); Battle of Lake Champlain (September 1814); Battle of Fort McHenry (September 1814); Battle of New Orleans (January 1815).

Armies:
    United States: The U.S. Army was small at the beginning of the war. It relied heavily on volunteers and state militias.

    Great Britain: British armies were well trained. But they also were fighting France and did not have many troops to battle the United States. Canadian militia and some American Indian tribes fought for the British.

Important Leaders:
    United States: General William Henry Harrison; General William Hull; Captain Isaac Hull; Commodore Oliver Hazard Perry; Colonel Richard Johnson; General Andrew Jackson; Captain Thomas Macdonough

    British: General Isaac Brock; Captain Philip Bowes Vere Broke; Sir George Prevost; Sir Edward Pakenham; General Robert Ross

    Weapons Used: Both sides used muskets, rifles, and cannons. Soldiers also attached bayonets to the ends of their muskets.

    End of War: The Treaty of Ghent was signed on December 24, 1814.

Chapter 1

Before the War

The United States gained its independence from Great Britain in the Revolutionary War (1775–1783). But many issues remained unsettled between these nations. Great Britain prevented U.S. trade overseas. Great Britain also tried to prevent U.S. expansion westward. Many U.S. leaders blamed the British for American Indians' refusal to give up their lands. These events eventually led to the War of 1812.

Westward Expansion
In 1803, Thomas Jefferson was president of the United States. He agreed to buy the Louisiana Territory from France. This land included the area between the Rocky Mountains in the west and the Mississippi River in the east.

President Thomas Jefferson hired Meriwether Lewis and William Clark to explore the Louisiana Territory.

William Henry Harrison led an attack against Prophetstown.

Jefferson hired Meriwether Lewis and William Clark to explore and map the Louisiana Territory. He gave Lewis and Clark instructions to meet the American Indians who already lived on this land. The U.S. government then made treaties with these peoples. The treaties promised American Indians money and goods in return for their land. But the U.S. government broke many of these promises.

Tecumseh was a powerful Shawnee leader. His brother the Prophet was a religious leader of these native people. They united many American Indian nations into a single confederacy. This union worked to stop settlers from moving west.

Tecumseh and the Prophet built a large village called Prophetstown in what is now Indiana. Tecumseh traveled around the country to speak to American Indians. He convinced many to join his confederacy and return to Prophetstown with him.

U.S. government leaders did not like the Indian Confederacy. They worried that the British were supplying American Indians with weapons. The U.S. government also was afraid that the American Indians might attack settlers.

In 1811, William Henry Harrison governed Indiana Territory. He attempted to break up the Indian Confederacy. Harrison led an army that attacked and burned Prophetstown. But this defeat did not stop Tecumseh. He continued to unite American Indians.

Foreign Conflicts

France and England often were at war during the late 1700s and early 1800s. In France, Napoleon Bonaparte was an ambitious ruler. He wanted to conquer Europe. Great Britain was a powerful nation that controlled many colonies. British leaders did not want to lose colonies or power to France. In 1792, these nations began a war that lasted more than 20 years.

British navy officers forced many U.S. sailors to serve on British ships.

Both France and England traded goods with the United States. Each country attempted to prevent the other from trading with the United States. But Great Britain's navy was more powerful than France's navy. British naval officers began to stop U.S. ships that they suspected were carrying goods to France.

British sailors were treated poorly at the time. These sailors received low pay and poor food. British sailors quickly grew tired of the war with

France. They began to desert. Many of these sailors who left the British Navy joined crews aboard U.S. ships. The conditions and pay were better on most U.S. ships.

The desertions angered British officials. British navy officers began to stop and board U.S. ships to look for deserters. The British officers sometimes impressed U.S. sailors. These sailors were wrongly taken from their ships and forced to serve in the British Navy.

Trade Laws

In 1807, the U.S. Congress passed the Embargo Act after a British ship attacked the U.S. frigate *Chesapeake*. This law prevented U.S. trade with foreign countries. Jefferson hoped an embargo would stop U.S. ships from getting into conflicts with foreign ships.

Many people in the United States complained about the Embargo Act. Southern farmers could not sell their crops to other countries. Northern traders could not buy or sell goods from foreign countries. In 1809, Congress decided to pass the Non-Intercourse Act. This law allowed trade with all countries except France and Great Britain.

Issues of the War

U.S. leaders had complaints against both Great Britain and France at the time. Both countries prevented U.S. trade overseas. But many issues still were unresolved with Great Britain from the Revolutionary War. For this reason, U.S. leaders favored war with Great Britain over France.

British ships continued to stop U.S. ships. By 1812, the British had impressed more than 10,000 U.S. sailors. British laws made it difficult for Americans to trade their goods overseas. U.S. leaders also feared that Great Britain was supplying American Indians with weapons.

In 1811, Congress included many young, new members from the South and the West. They were nicknamed the War Hawks. The War Hawks convinced many people that war with Great Britain was necessary. They said war was needed to improve relations with Great Britain and to defend the honor of the United States.

At the time, James Madison was president. He did not want to go to war. But pressure from the War Hawks affected his decision. In June 1812, Madison signed a declaration of war against Great Britain.

James Madison was president of the United States during the War of 1812.

Chapter 2

A Call to Arms

In 1812, the U.S. Army was small and poorly trained. It had less than 10,000 soldiers. Many of these soldiers had never fought in battle.

At the time, only men could be soldiers. They enlisted in the army for 5 years of service. They were promised incentives such as extra money and land to join the army. Soldiers also received monthly salaries. But the government often was behind in payments of these salaries.

At first, few men volunteered to join the army. The U.S. government then asked men to stay in the military only until the end of the war. It also offered more incentives. These offerings increased each year of the war and helped the army grow larger.

The U.S. Army needed more troops to fight a war against Great Britain.

State militia members also fought in the war. Men were more likely to join these local military groups than the U.S. Army. Militia members were not expected to leave their homes and families for long periods of time. They then could maintain their daily jobs and support their families.

The U.S. Navy

The United States had a small navy. It consisted of about 4,000 sailors and few warships. But most of these sailors were experienced. They also were good marksmen. The sailors fired cannons and muskets well.

Not many men enlisted in the U.S. Navy. Many more volunteers enlisted in the army to collect its incentives. Most sailors worked on privately owned ships. These sailors often made more money than those working for the navy.

The British Military

The British military was larger and more skilled than the U.S. military. But Great Britain also was at war with France. As a result, Great

U.S. soldiers wore blue coats with white pants.

Britain was not always able to send enough soldiers and ships to battle U.S. forces.

The British Navy was called the Royal Navy. It had more ships than any other country in the world. Sailors in the the Royal Navy were very skilled. At the time, the Royal Navy won most of its battles.

Uniforms and Weapons

British and U.S. soldiers wore similar uniforms. They wore short coats, white pants, and leather leggings over black shoes. The British soldiers wore red coats. U.S. soldiers wore blue coats.

During the War of 1812, the muzzle-loading musket was the main weapon. This gun fired a lead ball. Muskets could only hit targets that were about 100 yards (90 meters) away.

The U.S. Army required members of state militias to supply their own weapons. Many U.S. citizens owned rifles. They used these guns to hunt. They also used them during the war. Rifles often could shoot as far as 300 yards (270 meters). Their longer range proved to be a great advantage over British muskets.

Sailors fired cannons from warships.

Warships were equipped with cannons. Sailors used two types of cannons. Long guns had barrels 9 to 10 feet (2.7 to 3 meters) long. They could hit targets up to 1.5 miles (2.4 kilometers) away. Short guns were called carronades. They were 5 feet (1.5 meters) long. They could hit targets that were up to .5 miles (.8 kilometers) away.

Lake Superior

Lake Huron

Lake Michigan

Battle of the Thames

Detroit

Fort Malden

Fort Dearborn

Battle of Lake Erie

Prophetstown

St. Lawrence River
Montreal
Plattsburg
Lake Champlain
Lake Ontario
Sacket's Harbor
Fort Niagara
Lake Erie
Baltimore
Washington, D.C.
N
W
E
S

Chapter 3

Major Battles

Canada was a British colony at the time of the war. U.S. leaders planned to attack it. Four armies would strike Canada at the same time. The first three armies would separately attack Fort Niagara, Sacket's Harbor, and Plattsburg. These forts were on the border between New York and Canada. The three armies then would combine forces and attack Montreal, Quebec. The fourth army would attack Fort Malden near Lake Erie. U.S. military leaders were confident that they could easily defeat Canada. The British were busy fighting France and had few troops defending Canada.

The Fall of Detroit

U.S. General William Hull led 2,000 troops from Ohio to Detroit in the spring of 1812. He then

U.S. General William Hull surrendered Detroit to British forces.

Captain Isaac Hull's ship destroyed the British warship *Guerrière*.

planned to move into Canada and attack
Fort Malden. British General Isaac Brock
commanded a small force of Canadian militia
at Fort Malden. Tecumseh led a force of about
600 American Indians to help Brock.

The U.S. troops outnumbered Brock's forces.
But Brock and Tecumseh tricked Hull into
thinking they had more soldiers than they really
did. Tecumseh divided his men and marched
them around from different positions to make it

appear that Hull was surrounded. Brock dressed up his militia volunteers in red coats like those worn by British soldiers. Hull then thought he was up against well-trained British troops. He became too afraid to attack and he surrendered.

Battles at Sea

The first U.S. victory of the war came at sea. Captain Isaac Hull commanded the U.S. warship *Constitution*. He faced the British warship *Guerrière* off the Maine coast. The British sailors were firing their long-range cannons at the *Constitution*. They damaged the U.S. ship. But Hull waited to give his sailors the order to fire until they were in close range. They then fired all their guns at once and destroyed the British ship.

The United States did not always win at sea. In June 1813, the U.S. ship *Chesapeake* faced the British ship *Shannon* near Boston Harbor. James Lawrence commanded the *Chesapeake*. His sailors were inexperienced and poorly trained. They panicked when the British attacked. Lawrence was killed and the British won the battle.

Commodore Oliver Hazard Perry led U.S. sailors to victory in the Battle of Lake Erie.

The Battle of Lake Erie took place in September 1813. American Commodore Oliver Hazard Perry led a fleet of ships against the British. This group of ships included the *Lawrence* and the *Niagara*. Perry was aboard the *Lawrence*. During the battle, British long-range cannons caused much damage to the *Lawrence*. All of Perry's officers on board the *Lawrence* were killed or wounded.

The *Niagara* sailed behind the *Lawrence*. It had received little damage. Perry and several of his sailors on the *Lawrence* took a small boat to the *Niagara*. Perry continued to command his fleet from this ship. He forced the British fleet to surrender and took control of Lake Erie.

Battles with American Indians

In October 1813, two U.S. armies traveled toward Detroit. General William Henry Harrison and Colonel Richard Johnson led these armies. They forced the British to retreat to the east. The U.S. and British armies then battled on the banks of the Thames River in what is now Ontario.

Tecumseh led a group of American Indians to help the British. Harrison ordered Johnson's troops to attack Tecumseh's forces. Tecumseh was killed in the battle. After his death, many American Indians fled the battle site. The British troops then surrendered. The Battle of the Thames was considered a great U.S. victory. It put an end to the Indian Confederacy.

In the Mississippi Territory, Andrew Jackson defeated the Creeks in March 1814. This battle was called the Battle of Horseshoe Bend. It forced these American Indians to sign a treaty that gave part of their land to the United States.

The Creeks lost land in Georgia and what is now Alabama. The battle also ended American Indians' hope of keeping their land.

The Burning of Washington, D.C.
In 1814, Great Britain's war with France ended. Great Britain then could send more troops to fight against the United States.

In August 1814, about 4,000 British soldiers attacked Washington, D.C. Commodore Joshua Barney led a group of 400 U.S. soldiers against the British. They fought for nearly one-half hour. But the smaller U.S. force could not stop the British troops from advancing. The British set fire to the U.S. capitol building.

Battle of Lake Champlain
In September 1814, the Battle of Lake Champlain took place near Plattsburg, New York. The British ships outnumbered the U.S. ships nearly four to one. The British also had long-range cannons.

U.S. Captain Thomas Macdonough had four ships and 10 gunboats in his fleet. Macdonough arranged his ships in the narrow channel between Crab Island and Cumberland Head.

British troops captured and burned Washington, D.C.

This position kept the U.S. ships safe from British long-range cannons. It also forced the British ships to sail through a narrow stretch of water while under fire from U.S. cannons. Most of the British ships were seized or destroyed during the Battle of Lake Champlain.

Chapter 4

Life in Camp

Camp life for both U.S. and British soldiers was difficult. Soldiers often did not have enough food. Other supplies also ran low. U.S. troops sometimes went months without new shoes or blankets. Uniforms were too hot in the summer and not warm enough in the winter. Unclean conditions allowed diseases to spread through the camps.

Shelter

Soldiers often had to march between battle sites. At night, they looked for dry ground to sleep on. Soldiers rarely had tents or blankets. The soldiers got wet if it rained.

Soldiers marched between battle sites.

Permanent camps consisted of several buildings.

Soldiers stayed in battalions when they set up more permanent camps. This group of buildings often included a hospital and buildings to store ammunition and food rations. They also included kitchens and soldiers' living quarters.

Disease
Many diseases were common in soldiers' camps. Soldiers caught malaria, measles,

and smallpox. These diseases spread among the soldiers and killed thousands. Cold weather and lack of shelter and warm clothing also caused many cases of pneumonia in camps. This disease causes the lungs to fill with fluid and makes breathing difficult. Other diseases were caused by poor sanitary conditions. During the War of 1812, more soldiers died from diseases than were killed in battle.

Army surgeons cared for sick and wounded soldiers. At the time, these doctors did not have painkilling medicine for their patients. Instead, soldiers often drank alcohol before their operations.

During this time, surgeons did not know the importance of sterilizing their equipment to kill germs. Unclean operating equipment often caused wounds to become infected. Many patients died from infections they developed after their operations.

Chapter 5

The Final Battles

In September 1814, U.S. troops were preparing for battle. They strengthened the defenses around Baltimore, Maryland, and Fort McHenry. This fort was located on the Patapsco River near Baltimore. Soldiers dug trenches and built walls to make it more difficult for British soldiers to enter the city.

The British decided to attack Fort McHenry instead of Baltimore. They thought the defenses around Baltimore might be too difficult to defeat. U.S. sailors then sunk 24 ships in the Patapsco River. Most of the large British ships could not sail through the channel. But 16 smaller ships commanded by General Robert Ross managed

In September 1814, British forces attacked Fort McHenry.

to sail toward Fort McHenry. All night long, the British ships attacked the fort.

The next morning, the British stopped their attack. U.S. lawyer Francis Scott Key noticed that the U.S. flag was still flying above the fort. The flag meant that the British had not been successful in their attack. Soon afterward, the British Navy retreated. Key wrote the poem "The Defense of Fort McHenry" about this event. Later, this poem was set to music and became known as the "Star-Spangled Banner." This song became the U.S. national anthem in 1931.

A Treaty is Signed

Many U.S. and British leaders did not support the war between their countries. U.S. leaders did not feel their country was prepared for a war. Great Britain did not want to fight another war because they were already at war with France. As the fighting continued, these leaders sought to end the war.

News of the peace treaty was slow to reach the United States.

Evening Gazette Office,

The following most highly important handbill has just been issued from the CENTINEL press. We deem a duty that we owe our Friends and the Public to assist in the prompt spread of the Glorious News.

Treaty of PEACE signed and arrived.

CENTINEL Office. Feb. 13, 1815, 8 o'clock in the morning.

WE have this instant received in Thirty-two hours from New-York the following

Great and Happy News!

FOR THE PUBLIC.

To Benjamin Russell, *Esq. Centinel-Office, Boston.*

New-York, Feb. 11, 1815—Saturday Evening, 10 o'clock.

SIR—

I HASTEN to acquaint you, for the information of the Public, of the arrival here this afternoon of H. Br. M. sloop of war *Favorite*, in which has come passenger Mr. Carroll, American Messenger, having in his possession

A Treaty of Peace

Between this Country and Great-Britain, signed on the 26th December last.

Mr. Baker also is on board, as Agent for the British Government, the same who was formerly Charge des Affairs here.

Mr. Carroll reached town at eight o'clock this evening. He shewed to a friend of mine, who is acquainted with him, the pacquet containing the *Treaty*, and a London newspaper of the last date of December, announcing the signing of the Treaty

It depends, however, as my friend observed, upon the act of the President to suspend hostilities on this side.

The gentleman left London the 2d Jan. The *Transit* had sailed previously from a port on the Continent.

This city is in a perfect uproar of joy, shouts, Illuminations, &c. &c.

I have undertaken to send you this by Express—the rider engaging to deliver it by Eight o'clock on Monday morning. The expense will be 225 dollars :—If you can collect so much to indemnify me I will thank you to do so.

I am with respect, Sir, your obedient servant,

JONATHAN GOODHUE.

We most heartily felicitate our Country on this auspicious news, which may be relied on as wholly authentic—Centinel.

PEACE EXTRA.

Peace talks between the United States and Great Britain began in August 1814. On December 24, 1814, British and U.S. officials signed a peace treaty in Ghent, Belgium. The treaty stated that all prisoners would be released and that territory captured during the war would be returned. But the treaty did not solve any of the issues that began the war.

Battle of New Orleans

News of the treaty was slow to reach the United States. It had to be carried overseas by ship and often took weeks to reach people in the United States. One battle was fought two weeks after the treaty was signed. During this battle, the soldiers did not realize that the war was over.

In January 1815, British General Edward Pakenham led 50 ships into the Gulf of Mexico. The ships carried about 7,500 troops. He planned to attack New Orleans, Louisiana.

U.S. General Andrew Jackson quickly put together an army. He brought in soldiers from

The Battle of New Orleans occurred after the War of 1812 was over.

Tennessee, Kentucky, and Louisiana to defend New Orleans. He also recruited the help of pirate Jean Lafitte.

On January 8, 1815, Pakenham led his army against the U.S. forces. But Jackson's soldiers were prepared. Nearly 2,000 British soldiers were killed or wounded within the first half-hour of fighting. The British quickly retreated. Fewer than 100 Americans lost their

Andrew Jackson (1767–1845)

Jackson was born March 15, 1767, on the border between North and South Carolina. At age 13, he joined the army and fought in the Revolutionary War (1775–1783) against the British. In 1787, Jackson was appointed as prosecuting officer for the Superior Court in Nashville, Tennessee. He was elected to the House of Representatives (1796–1797). He also served in the Senate (1797–1798). In 1802, Jackson was elected a major general of the Tennessee militia. He fought in the War of 1812 and was promoted to general in 1814. Jackson served two terms as president (1829–1837). He later retired to his home near Nashville. He died June 8, 1845.

lives during the battle. Jackson become a national hero because of this victory.

The End of the War
On February 11, 1815, news about the peace treaty reached New York. In churches, bells rang. In citizens' homes, candles were lit. People cheered in the streets.

The War of 1812 did not bring a great deal of change for either Great Britain or the United States. But after the war, these two nations were on friendlier terms. They never went to war again. This war also helped the United States gain respect as a nation from other countries around the world.

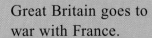
Timeline

Great Britain goes to
war with France.

James Madison is
elected president of
the United States.

1792

1808

1807

1811

William Henry
Harrison leads an
attack against
Prophetstown. This
battle is known as the
Battle of Tippecanoe.

The *Chesapeake* is
attacked by the
British ship *Leopard*;
U.S. Congress passes
the Embargo Act.

March—Battle of Horseshoe Bend takes place.

June—U.S. leaders declare war on Great Britain.

July—British forces capture Detroit.

August—U.S. *Constitution* battles the British warship *Guerrière*.

August—British forces capture Washington, D.C., and burn the U.S. capitol building.

September—Battles of Lake Champlain and Fort McHenry occur.

December—U.S. and British leaders sign Treaty of Ghent.

1812

1814

1813

1815

June—*Chesapeake* battles the British ship *Shannon*.

September—Battle of Lake Erie takes place.

October—Battle of Thames occurs.

January—Battle of New Orleans takes place after the War of 1812 is over.

Words to Know

battalion (buh-TAL-yun)—a large group of soldiers

confederacy (kuhn-FED-ur-uh-see)—a union of people or groups with a common goal

enlist (ehn-LIST)—to join the military

impress (im-PRESS)—to force a person to do something; British naval officers often impressed American sailors into serving in the British Navy.

militia (muh-LISH-uh)—a group of civilians who serve as soldiers in emergencies

musket (MUHSS-kit)—a gun with a long barrel; muskets were commonly used during the War of 1812.

treaty (TREE-tee)—an agreement between two or more groups; treaties often end conflicts between two nations.

To Learn More

Bosco, Peter I. *The War of 1812.* Brookfield, Conn.: Millbrook Press, 1991.

Collier, Christopher and James Lincoln Collier. *The Jeffersonian Republicans, 1800–1823: The Louisiana Purchase and the War of 1812.* Drama of American History. New York: Benchmark Books, 1999.

Gay, Kathlyn and Martin Gay. *War of 1812.* Voices from the Past. New York: Twenty-First Century Books, 1995.

Quiri, Patricia Ryon. *The National Anthem.* A True Book. New York: Children's Press, 1998.

Useful Addresses

Battlefield House Museum
P.O. Box 66561
Stoney Creek, ON L8G 5E5
Canada

**Fort McHenry National Monument and
 Historic Shrine**
End of East Fort Avenue
Baltimore, MD 21230-5393

Naval Historical Center
Washington Navy Yard
805 Kidder Breese SE
Washington, DC 20374-5060

Star-Spangled Banner Flag House
844 E. Pratt Street
Baltimore, MD 21202

Internet Sites

The History of Tecumseh and the Battle at Tippecanoe Creek
http://www.tippecanoe.com/corp/tec_hist.html

The War of 1812
http://www.multied.com/1812

War of 1812–1814
http://members.tripod.com/~war1812

The War of 1812 Website
http://www.militaryheritage.com/1812.htm

Index